Juvenile
SCHAUMBURG TOWNSHIP DISTRICT LIBRARY
W9-BGE-915
Schaumburg Township District Library
130 South Roselle Road
Schaumburg, Illinois 60193

Rama and Sita

For Linda

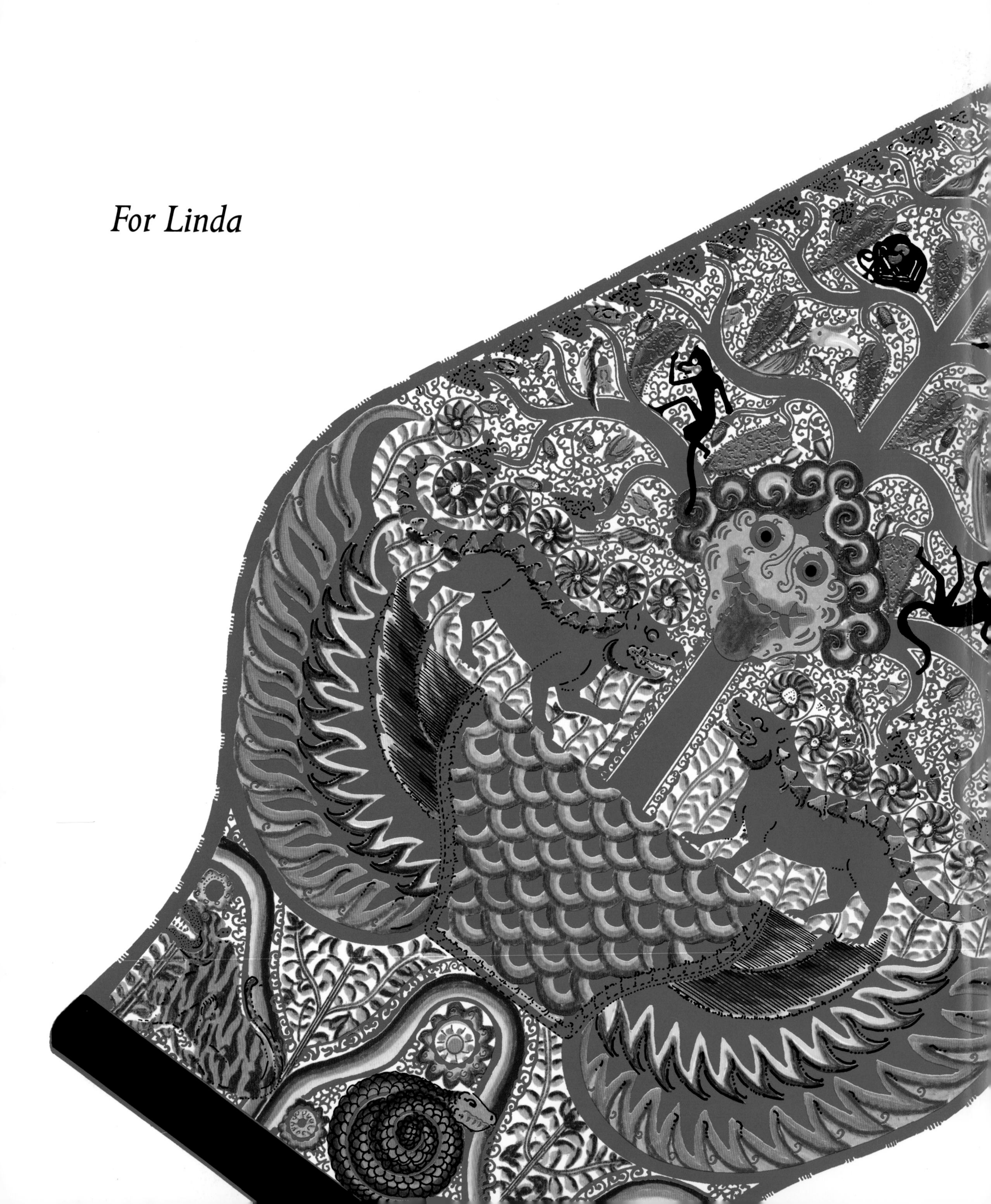

Rama and Sita

A Tale from Ancient Java

Retold and Illustrated by

David Weitzman

DAVID R. GODINE ✦ Publisher ✦ Boston

Tell us again the old story, the children ask. Sing for us the *Ramayana*, the tale of prince Rama, of his love for Sita, and his wild adventures with Hanuman, King of the Monkeys.

So the *dalang*, the story teller, lovingly sets out his golden puppets in the way it was done by his father and his father's father. In his hands each little figure comes alive in fluttering shadows on a white cloth lit by an oil lamp sun. To his left, gods and noble princes, learned and gentle, who must also be fierce warriors. For arrayed against them is all the evil in the world — savage ogres and brutish red-eyed giants. Now they stand in the flickering light, awaiting their turn to enter the world of the dancing shadows.

The ancient story, that will continue long into the night, until dawn, now begins.

Our story opens in a fabled kingdom long, long ago,
a peaceful place of tree-shaded paths and thatched-roof houses.
Gardenia and jasmine blossoms scent the warm days
and nights, and everywhere water delights the ear,
trickling,
rippling,
bubbling,
trilling,
splashing,
cascading down
from terrace
to terrace of
silvery rice
fields

lying on the hills like broken pieces of mirror filled with blue sky and clouds. The streams become rivers swirling around gentle gray water buffalo, like islands, each with a child on its broad back and rings of silver on its horns. Saffron banners flutter above busy markets and street festivals of music, dance, and song.

The ruler was a noble, old king, Dasarata, who knew by heart the laws and sacred writings. He was just and fair, and he never, never forgot a promise. Dasarata's greatest loves were his three sons, Rama, Lesmana, and Barata, the youngest. They were, everyone agreed, like mirror images of their father, brave and wise, and kind, like four stars of a heavenly constellation.

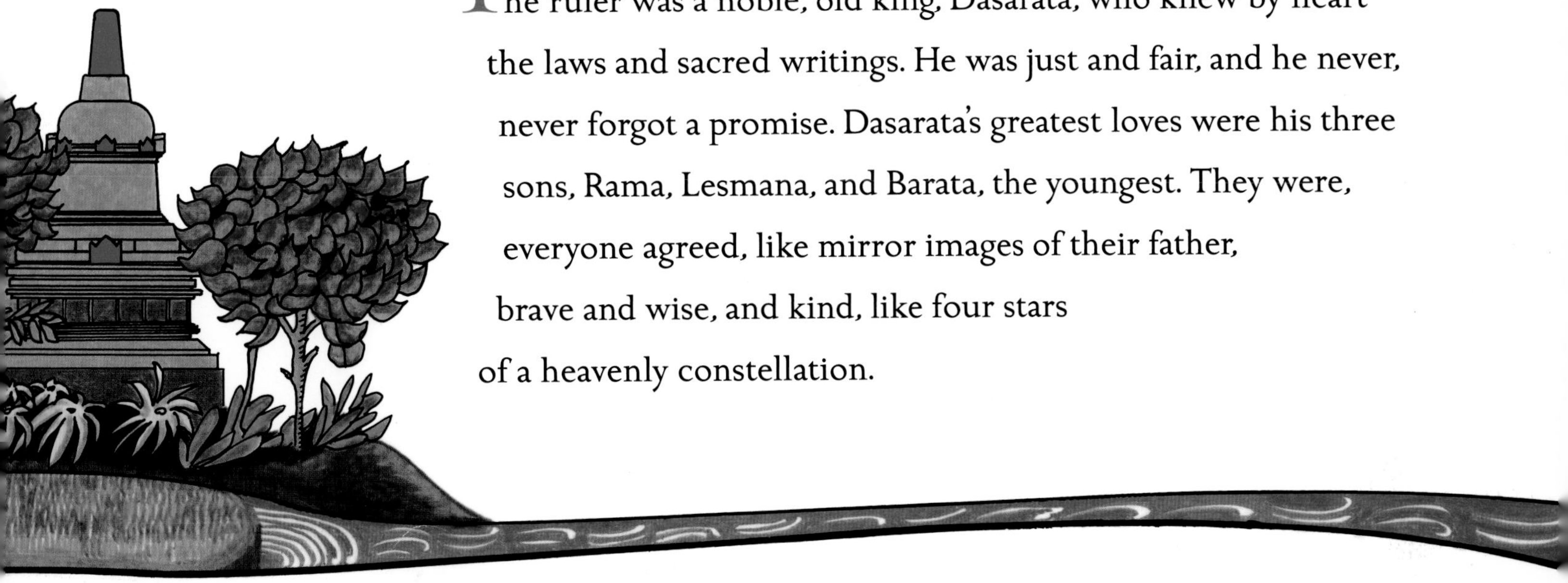

But Dasarata knew the end of his life was near. There had been ominous signs; a giant would have swallowed the moon had the people not scared him away with their loud shouting. And stars were falling from the heavens. So he called together his councilors from far and wide, and told them his wish: "Before I die, I would like see my son rule."

"Then let your first born, Rama, be our king," the people cheered. "Rama, Rama, blessed with a dancer's grace and a warrior's prowess," they chanted. "Rama, Rama, gallant prince," their voices echoed from the snowy mountain tops to the green valleys. Let preparations for the coronation and celebration begin!

The streets were strewn with blossoms and to the creator of the universe was sent rare incense. Tomorrow Rama and Sita will be king and queen. The people danced to songs of flutes and drums, and everywhere there was happiness — except in the palace deep in one dark, tormented heart.

Why should Rama be king?" Barata's mother seethed, her soul aflame with envy. "Why not *my* dear son instead? Surely, he is as brave as Rama, and as wise. And if he were king, then I would be the mother honored above all others." "Barata will be king," she hissed, "and I will see to it." So that very night she went to the king in tears.

"Remember when you lay dying on the battlefield, and I healed your wounds and restored you to life?"

"Will you honor my wishes now, tonight?"

"Then tomorrow make my son Barata king, and banish Rama to the forest for fourteen years."

"You must grant my wishes. You promised as you lay dying. . ."

"Remember, if you do not keep your word, your name and your sons' names will be tarnished for all time. Your people will stray from the honorable path you have shown them."

"My dear queen, what pains you so? Tell me, and I will do all that is in my power to make you happy again."

"How could I ever forget? And for that I promised you two wishes."

"Of course, I will, true to my word."

"No, no!"

"No, no I cannot. I cannot. . ."

"Rama, oh Rama, I cannot take back my word."

Night turned to morning, but for Dasarata no sun dawned that day. The king summoned Rama with a broken heart and told him what must be. Always the dutiful son, Rama bade his father farewell, and then went to his brother.

But Lesmana would not say farewell. "Since we were boys, I have always been at your side. And so I will be on this journey." Sita, too, would not let her husband go alone. "I must share your fate," she told him. "As you walk the path through darkness and evil, I will be at your side." And Barata? Wanting no part of his mother's treachery, he pleaded with Rama to stay and become their king. "No, Barata," Rama insisted, "you must stay, because that is our father's decree."

And so that day they set out — Rama, Sita, and Lesmana — on a journey which took them over mountains, across wild, roaring rivers, deep into the vast forest that would be their home.

The next morning the travelers awoke to a familiar voice calling out to them. It was Barata. "Our father, the king, has died of a broken heart," he told them. "Now, Rama, you are no longer bound by your promise and may return to rule the kingdom."

"Dear Barata, you must be king," Rama insisted, "and I must remain here in the forest to honor our father's word, even more so now that he is dead." So they sat down together and Rama instructed his youngest brother in the duties of a king. "Keep to the righteous path. Heed the advice of your councilors, for they are old and wise. And to each citizen give ear. You are just and true and of generous soul, dear Barata. You will rule well."

And with this, Rama bowed before him and, removing his magic sandals, placed them on the young lord's feet. After filling his eyes and his heart with the faces of his exiled brothers, Barata returned to rule their kingdom.

Our heroes spent their days gathering mangoes, and bananas, and pineapples and meditating in the dappled sunlight under trees of fragrant blossoms. During the cool nights Rama and Sita slept on a bed of soft mosses Lesmana had made for them under a sheltering bower of purple morning glory vines.

Still, danger is close by. From the thickets come eerie sounds in the night and flashes of demon light. This very moment, hidden in the forest gloom, Ravana, King of the Rakasas, watches their every move, especially the lotus-eyed Sita. He thinks of nothing but capturing her for his own, and he schemes to get Rama and Lesmana away. Sita is safely beyond his grasp, protected by a magic circle Rama has drawn with his dagger. "As long as you remain within this circle," he assures Sita, "no harm can come to you." And so, secure in the brothers' protection, she gathers flowers in the meadow and plays with the animals that come to visit her.

One day there comes a deer more beautiful than any she had ever seen, with skin like polished gold and eyes of violet amethyst. "Quick, my lord, come see," Sita calls out, and begs Rama to catch the deer for her. Though he does not want to leave Sita's side, Rama agrees.

Stay with Sita, Lesmana, and do not
let her leave the circle." Rama gathers
up his bow and quiver, and goes off to
catch the golden deer, leaping,
bounding before him,
now quiet in a sunny glade,
now vanished into the wood,
head down nibbling grasses,
gleaming golden in the sun
like a jewel
beckoning Rama
deep,
deep,
deep into the forest,
farther and farther away from Sita.
Then the deer comes to rest, stone still,
as if awaiting the hunter's approach. Rama
sees other deer run from it, and something
in its shimmering, shifting outline alerts him.
He draws his bow and his arrow strikes
deep into the golden heart. But in death
it is not a golden deer but devilry sent by
Ravana to lure Rama away from Sita.
With its last breath the deer calls out,
"Help me, Lesmana, help me!"
in a voice that sounds
just like
Rama's.

Lesmana, fly, fly to Rama's side," Sita cries, her lover's screams still echoing in her ears. But Lesmana knows it is an evil trick. "I cannot leave you here alone, Sita, that was Rama's order."

"Go, Lesmana, hasten to the wood where Rama surely needs you."

Despite his fears, Lesmana runs toward the voice in the distance, disappearing into the wood, leaving Sita alone.

No sooner has Lesmana gone then there appears a wizened little man in a tattered gray hermit's cloak, begging for a sip of water. "Come refresh your soul," she bids him, "and for a while, ancient one, be our honored guest."

Sita steps out of the magic circle. Suddenly the sun dims, the wind falls silent as though the world dare not breathe. The cloak falls away, and out of the stooped figure arises a giant terrible as death, with ten heads and twenty arms, eyes ablaze with red fire. "I am Ravana, King of the Rakasas, and I will take you beyond the sea to be my queen."

Two of Ravana's immense hands grab her long hair, four of his arms encircle her waist, four more lift her off her feet, and he whisks her up into the clouds, black as ashes, to his kingdom far, far away.

High over the tree tops they fly like a windstorm, Sita struggling in Ravana's crushing grip. When the brothers return they find the circle empty, and Sita's cries are too distant to be heard. Dazed and fearful, Rama and Lesmana set out to find Sita. But where to look?

Jathayu, King of the Birds, does hear Sita's cries and, taking flight on great wings, soars to her rescue. With talons as big as elephant tusks he attacks, wheeling, swooping, parrying the storm of keen-pointed arrows loosed from Ravana's ten bows. Jathayu rips the giant's flesh, tears away ten arms, and crushes the bows in his beak. Ravana, eyes rolling in fury, his body shuddering with pain, draws his terrible sword and plunges it deep into Jathayu's breast. Jathayu plummets to earth with a clap of thunder. And there he lies, crumpled and broken, struggling against death, so that he can tell someone of Sita's fate.

Searching for Sita, the brothers find the wounded Jathayu. Rama lowers his ear to the feathered breast and a faintly beating heart. Feeling the gentle strokes on his wing, Jathayu opens his eyes. "The fair lady you seek is Ravana's captive borne swiftly away..." and life passes out of Jathayu there in Rama's arms. The brothers gather wood and, lighting the pyre, mourn their friend, honoring in death the great warrior bird, blessing his spirit to heaven with fire.

Flying on the wind, Ravana takes Sita far to the south. Seeing some monkeys on a mountain top below she lets fall

a silver anklet,

golden earrings,

necklace,

and chain, which come to rest on the mountain peak like fallen stars. The monkeys take the glittering trinkets to their king, Hanuman, Son of the Wind. Meanwhile, the brothers have searched through dark woods and caves, crossing raging rivers and thundering waterfalls until, finally, they too have reached the monkey kingdom. Hanuman shows Rama what the monkeys have found, and recognizing them as Sita's, he tells the Monkey King of his wife's capture by the terrible Ravana.

"Grieve not, dear Rama," Hanuman says, wiping the warrior's tears, "I will help you." And with that Hanuman orders his monkey armies to combat. Monkey messengers summon their brothers from cloud-capped peaks, from the forests east and west, north and south, urging them to come with utmost speed. And they come. Three million monkey warriors fierce and strong, ten millions brave and bold.

Hanuman leaps through the clouds on a whirlicane, bearing Rama's golden ring to Sita as proof that help is on the way. And a tidal wave of leaping, bounding monkeys speeds south. But when at last the monkey armies reach the southern sea and face the surging tempest pounding the shore, it seems they can go no farther. What to do? Angry, feeling hopeless, one monkey heaves a rock mightily into the water, and then another throws a rock, and another, and another, then scores, then a hundred, then thousands, then millions of monkeys are hurling immense boulders into the churning waters until a stone road bridges the sea all the way to Ravana's kingdom.

Alarmed by the clamor of monkeys crossing the sea, armies of lumbering giants stream from the city gates . . . only to find a silent, empty forest. Then suddenly a thousand million shrieks pierce the air, and the trees come alive with fierce monkey warriors, clambering up the giant's legs and arms, onto their shoulders, biting their noses and ears, chins and cheeks, fingers and toes, sending them fleeing back over the city walls, pursued by monkeys, millions of monkeys, filling the moat with stones and boulders, leaping from tower to tower, from gate to parapet, striking down the ogres with fist and hand and golden arrows like meteors.

His army cowering in fear and his city in flames, Ravana turns to his only hope, the mighty giant, Kumbakarna. In an instant Kumbakarna is over the wall with one easy bound. Beneath his feet the earth shudders, glaciers rumble down from the mountains and it seems as if the stars and planets might fall.

With trembling hearts the monkeys
scatter and flee to the forest,
leaving only Lesmana
between Rama
and certain death.
Dodging,
ducking,
darting,
weaving,
skipping,
feinting between the deadly tramping feet,
Lesmana lets fly from his bow
a magic arrow
on a lightning bolt.
Kumbakarna staggers
and crashes to the ground like
an avalanche of boulders.

Now Rama hunts down Ravana, on his bowstring an arrow from the gods. There is the demon king, cringing behind a wall. Rama draws his mighty bow and sends his arrow, fiery and furious as a solar wind,
piercing Ravana's chest
and cleaving his heart.

Suddenly, the birds begin to sing,
the sun brightens, a soft breeze
rustles in the trees, and from the sky
falls a gentle rain of white blossoms.

The world is at peace again.
The years of exile have passed. It is time to go home.
So Hanuman gathers up Rama, Sita, and Lesmana in his arms
and whisks them on the wind back to their kingdom, where,
riding atop the grandest elephant in all the kingdom,
they enter the city's gates floating in a sea of
monkey warriors arrayed in golden cloth.
A rainbow of banners flutters and snaps in the wind,
and in the streets are joyful crowds dancing to the merry
sounds of flutes and drums, chanting "Rama, Rama."

Barata greets them at the palace and
places the magic sandals once again
on Rama's feet. "My king and dear brother,"
he announces for all to hear, "you are now lord
of our land, and all is right again."
From that day on, and for ten thousand years,
Rama ruled wisely, defending all that
was just and fair. Never, never did
he forget a promise. And for this
he will be revered and loved
and remembered until
the end of time.

The *dalang* takes up the tree of life
which began the story, and spins it into
a twirling shadow like the fluttering of wings.
Harmony has been restored to the world,
and the storyteller's task is done.

After a moment's rest and meditation, he carefully returns the puppets to their wooden box, covers them with a cloth, and offers a prayer. The audience stirs to life, bids one another *selamat pagi,* may your morning be blessed. Parents awaken their sleepy children and, in a joyous murmur drift out into the sun-warmed morning.